KURT WOLFF VERLAG / MÜNCHEN

Das neue Buch von Franz Kafka

EIN LANDARZT

Kleine Erzählungen von
FRANZ KAFKA

192 Seiten Groß-Oktav in besonders vornehmer Ausstattung

Preis geheftet M. 12.—, Halbleder M. 40.—
Ab 1. Dezember kein Verlags-Teuerungszuschlag

Aus dem ersten Urteil:

„Diese Aufzeichnungen traumhafter Begebenheiten sind der selten ge-
glückte Versuch deutscher Literatur, abstraktestes Geschehen kon-
kretest zu sagen. — Stilproben, in denen kein Wort entfallen, keines
hinzugesetzt werden dürfte, wenn nicht der Bau zusammenstürzen
soll, von allen Ismen freigebliebene, peinlich saubere deutsche Prosa:
das äußere Gewand. Gebändigte Phantasie, dahinter tausendfache
Bedeutung, die man nur ahnen darf: der sogenannte „Inhalt". Beides
zusammen ergibt als Wirkung Herzklopfen, atemloses Interesse und,
als Wertvollstes, bei jenen Lesern Nachdenklichkeit, auf deren Kreis
allein es einem Dichter ankommen kann, der Sätze niederschreibt,
wie solche, die sich, ein wundervolles Bild auch rein äußerlich, über
ganze Seiten des neuen Buches ranken. Man merke
es sich, noch einmal sei es genannt: Franz Kafka
‚Ein Landarzt' (bei Kurt Wolff)."
Prager Tagblatt.

Hauptauslieferungslager bei F. Volckmar in Leipzig

VITALIS

BIBLIOTHECA
BOHEMICA

A COUNTRY DOCTOR

Franz Kafka

A Country Doctor

Short Stories

To my father

VITALIS

© Vitalis 2007 • Bibliotheca Bohemica • Cover design and illustrations by Karel Hruška • Translated from the German by Siegfried Mortkowitz • Afterword on the creation and impact of the text by Elisabeth Fuchs, translated by Rachel Ward • Printed and bound in the European Union ISBN 978-80-7253-235-3 • All rights reserved
www.vitalis-verlag.com

The publishers would like to thank Mr Hartmut Binder for permission to print the illustration on page 95 from his archive material. The remaining pictorial material is taken from the publisher's own archive of photographs and historical publications.

CONTENTS

THE NEW ATTORNEY

We have a new attorney, Dr Bucephalus. There is little in his appearance that recalls the time when he was still Alexander of Macedonia's warhorse. Those familiar with the circumstances, however, will notice a thing or two. Why, not long ago I saw, outside on the steps, even a simple court usher admire the attorney with the professional glance of a racetrack regular as he climbed the stairs, kicking high his legs, with a step that made the marble ring.

In general, the Bar approves of Bucephalus' admission. They tell themselves, with astonishing insight, that Bucephalus is in a difficult position in today's society and therefore, and because of his historical significance, he deserves some obligingness. Today – and this no one can deny – there is no Alexander the Great. Of course, some know how to murder; there is also no lack of skill in spearing a friend across a banquet table; and for many Macedonia is too cramped, so that they curse Philip, his father – but no one, no one is able to march on India. Even back in those days India's gates were beyond reach, but the King's sword indicated their direction. Today, the gates stand in totally different places, farther away and higher up; no one shows the way; many hold swords, but only to brandish them; and the eye that tries to follow them grows confused.

Perhaps that is why it is really best, as Bucephalus has done, to immerse oneself in law books. Free, his flanks unhampered by the rider's loins, at a peaceful lamp, far from the tumult of Alexander's battle, he reads and turns the pages of our ancient books.

A Country Doctor

I was in a dire predicament: an urgent journey
lay before me; a gravely ill patient awaited me
in a village ten miles away; a heavy snowfall
filled the vast space between me and him;
I had a light carriage with large wheels perfectly suited to our highways; wrapped in my
fur coat, medical bag in hand, I was standing
in the courtyard ready for the journey; but
the horse was lacking, the horse. My own
horse had died the previous night because it
had worked too hard this icy winter; my servant-girl was now running around the village
looking to borrow a horse; but it was hopeless,
I knew it and, increasingly covered by snow,
growing more and more motionless, I stood
there doing nothing. The girl appeared at the
gate, alone, swinging the lantern; of course,
who would lend out his horse now for such
a journey? I paced across the courtyard again;
nothing came to me; distracted, I kicked in
anguish at the splintering door of the pigsty,
which had not been used for years. It opened
and swung back and forth on its hinges.
Warmth and an odour like that of horses
wafted out. Inside, a dim lantern swayed on
a rope. Cowering in the low shed, a man presented his frank, blue-eyed visage. "Shall I
hitch up?" he asked, crawling forward on all
fours. I didn't know what to say, and merely
crouched to see what else there was in the

stall. The servant-girl stood beside me. "You never know what things there are in your own household," she said, and we both laughed. "Hey, Brother; hey, Sister!" the groom cried and, one after the other, two horses, powerful beasts with muscular flanks, their legs close to their bodies, hanging their well-formed heads like camels, thrust themselves by the mere force of their swinging rumps through the door opening, which they filled completely. But soon they stood erect, long-legged, their bodies giving off dense steam. "Help him," I said, and the compliant girl hurried to hand the harness to the groom. Yet she has hardly reached him when he grabs her and presses his face against hers. She cries out and flees back to me; two rows of teeth are engraved in red in the girl's cheek. "You beast," I scream furiously, "do you want a whipping?" but immediately remember that he is a stranger; that I don't know where he comes from and that he is helping me voluntarily when everyone else has failed me. As if he can read my thoughts, he takes no offence at my threat but, constantly occupied with the horses, turns toward me just once. "Get in," he says then, and in fact: everything is ready. With such a beautiful team of horses – this I notice – I have never ridden, and I cheerfully climb on. "But I will drive, you don't know the way," I say. "Certainly," he says, "I'm not coming along, I'm staying with Rosa." "No," Rosa shrieks and, correctly foreseeing the inevitability of her fate, runs into the house; I hear the rattle of the door chain that she fastens; I hear the lock click into place; I see how in the hallway and fleeing through the rooms, she also turns off all the lights to make herself impossible to find. "You're coming along," I tell the groom, "or I won't make the trip, no matter how urgent it is. I don't have the slightest intention of giving you the girl as payment for the journey." "Giddy-up!" he says; claps his hands; the wagon is swept forward like a log in a current; I can still hear the door to my house burst and splinter under the groom's assault, then my eyes and ears are filled with a roar that penetrates all my senses with equal force. But this also for just a moment because, as if my patient's courtyard lay just outside my own gate, I am already there; the horses stand quietly; it has stopped snowing; moonlight all around; the invalid's parents rush out of the house; his sister behind them; I am almost lifted bodily out of the carriage; I understand nothing of their confused jabber; the air in the sickroom is scarcely fit for breathing; the neglected stove smoulders; I will open the window; but first I want to see my patient. Thin, no fever, not cold, not warm, with blank eyes, shirtless, the young man lifts himself up under the eiderdown, clings to my neck, whispers in my ear: "Doctor, let me die." I look around; no one heard him; the parents lean forward silently and await my judgement; the sister has brought a chair for my bag. I open

the bag and search among my instruments; the young man keeps reaching for me from the bed to remind me of his plea; I grab a pair of forceps, inspect them in the candlelight and put them down again. "Yes," I think blasphemously, "in cases like this the gods are obliging, send the missing horse, add a second because of the urgency, and to top it all even donate a groom –" Only now do I think of Rosa again; what do I do, how shall I save her, how do I get her out from under that groom when I am ten miles away and with unruly horses hitched to my rig? These horses, which have somehow loosened the reins; which, I don't know how, are pushing open the windows from outside; each one sticks its head through a window and, unruffled by the family's outcry, observes the invalid. "I'll drive back soon," I think, as if the horses were summoning me to the journey, but I allow the sister, who thinks that I am dazed from the heat, to remove my fur coat. A glass of rum is poured for me, the old man claps me on the shoulder, the offer of his treasure justifies this intimacy. I shake my head; I am feeling sick in the narrow confines of the old man's thinking; this is the only reason I refuse to drink. The mother stands at the bedside and beckons to me; I comply and, as a horse whinnies noisily at the ceiling, lay my head on the boy's breast, and he shivers under my wet beard. This confirms what I already know: the boy is healthy, his circulation is a bit weak, saturated with coffee by the caring mother, but healthy and best driven out of bed with a shove. I'm no do-gooder, and let him lie there. I am employed by the district and do my duty to the hilt, to the point where it is almost too much. Badly paid, I am nevertheless generous and helpful to the poor. I also have to care for Rosa, so perhaps the boy is right, and I want to die too. What am I doing here in this endless winter! My horse has died, and there is no one in the village who will lend me his. I have to drag my team out of the pigsty; if they hadn't by chance been horses, I would have had to travel with swine. That's how it is. And I nod at the family. They know nothing about it, and if they did know, they wouldn't believe it. To write prescriptions is easy, but to communicate with people is difficult. Well, here my visit should be over, once again I've been called out for nothing, I'm used to that, the entire district torments me with the help of my night bell, but that this time I also had to abandon Rosa, this beautiful girl who, scarcely noticed by me, has lived in my house for years – this sacrifice is too great, and I have to split hairs to come to terms with it in my head so as not to lay into this family, who try as they might cannot give Rosa back to me. But when I shut my bag and motion for my fur coat, the family standing together, the father snivelling over the glass of rum in his hand, the mother, probably disappointed by me – well, what do people expect? – tearfully biting her lips and the sister waving a blood-soaked towel, I am somehow willing, under certain conditions, to admit that the boy might be ill after all. I go toward him, he smiles at me as if I were bringing him the strongest of soups – oh, now the two horses are whinnying; I guess the noise, arranged by higher authorities, is supposed to facilitate the examination – and now I find: yes, the boy is ill. In his right side, near his hip, a wound as big as the palm of my hand has opened. Rose-coloured, of various shades, dark in the cavities, growing lighter at the edges, softly granular, with unevenly pooling blood, open to daylight like a surface mine. That's how it is from a distance. Close up, another complication appears. Who can look at this without giving a soft whistle? Worms as thick and long as my little finger, rose-coloured and blood-spattered on top of that, with white heads and many legs, wriggle towards the light while fastened to the interior of the wound. Poor boy, you're beyond help. I have discovered your great wound; this flower in your side will be the death of you. The family is happy, they see me at work; the sister tells the mother, the mother tells the father, the father tells several guests who come into the room on tiptoe, passing through the moonlight at the open door, stretching out their arms for balance. "Are you going to save me?" whispers the boy, sobbing, overcome by the life in his open wound. That's how the people are in my neck

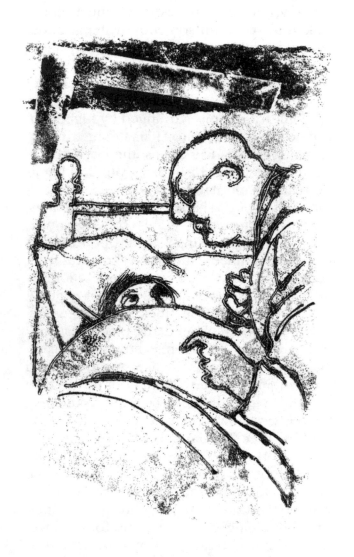

of the woods. Always asking their doctor for the impossible. They've lost the old beliefs; the pastor sits at home and pulls apart his stole and chasuble, one after the other; but the doctor is supposed to rectify everything with his gentle surgical hand. Well, whatever you want: I haven't forced my services on you; if you use me for sacred ends, I'll let that happen, too; what do I want more, old country doctor that I am, robbed of my servant-girl! And here they come, the family and the village elders, and undress me; a school choir, with the teacher at its head, stands in front of the house and sings a very simple melody to the words:

"Undress him, then he will cure,
And if he doesn't cure, kill him!
's just a doctor, 's just a doctor."

Then I am undressed and, with my fingers in my beard, my head bowed, calmly look at the people. I am altogether composed and on top of things, and remain so even though it doesn't help me at all, because now they take me by the head and feet and carry me to the bed. They lay me against the wall, on the side the wound is on. Then they all leave the room; the door is shut; the singing ceases; clouds pass over the moon; the bedding is warm around me; the horses' heads sway like shadows in the open windows. "You know," I hear said in my ear, "I have very little confidence in you. You're also nothing but a cast-off, you're not here on your own. Instead of helping, you make my deathbed smaller for me. I'd love to scratch your eyes out." "Right," I say, "it's a disgrace. But I'm a doctor. What am I supposed to do? Believe me, it's not easy for me either." "I'm supposed to content myself with this explanation? Ah, I guess I'll have to. I always have to make do. I came into the world with a nice wound; that was my entire outfit." "Young man," I say, "your mistake is: you have no perspective. I, who have already been in all the sickrooms far and wide, say to you: your wound is not so terrible. Made with two blows of the axe at a sharp angle. Many offer up their sides and scarcely hear the axe in the forest, let alone that it comes anywhere near them." "Is it really like that or are you trying to hoodwink me in my fever?" "It's really like that, take a medical officer's word of honour." And he took it and fell silent. But now it was time to think about my rescue. The horses were still standing faithfully in their places. Clothing, fur coat and bag were hastily gathered up; I didn't want to waste my time getting dressed; if the horses were to run the way they did on the way here, I could jump out of this bed and into my own, so to speak. A horse withdrew obediently from the window; I threw the bundle onto the rig; the fur coat flew too far, clung to a hook by just one sleeve. Good enough. I swung myself onto the horse. The reins loosely trailing, one horse scarcely tied to the other, the buggy struggling along behind, the fur coat trailing in the snow.

"Giddy-up!", I said, but that was hardly the effect; we moved through the snowy waste as slowly as old men; for a long time, the new but erroneous singing of the children echoed behind us:

"Rejoice, you patients,
The doctor has put you to bed!"

I will never reach home this way; my flourishing practice is lost; my successor is stealing from me, but in vain, for he cannot replace me; in my house the loathsome groom is raging; Rosa is his victim; I don't want to think about it. Naked, exposed to the frost of this most calamitous age, with an earthly carriage, unearthly horses, I, an old man, roam about. My fur coat is hanging from the back of the carriage, but I can't reach it, and not one of my agile riff-raff patients lifts a finger. Betrayed! Betrayed! There's no way back once you've answered the false alarm of the night bell.

In the Gallery

If some frail, consumptive equestrienne on a lurching horse were driven round and round in circles in the circus ring by a pitiless, whip-cracking ringmaster for months on end without a pause in front of an insatiable audience, whizzing around on the horse, throwing kisses, rocking back and forth from the waist, and if this game were to continue into the ceaselessly unfolding grey future to the uninterrupted din of the orchestra and ventilators, accompanied by the slackening and renewed swelling of clapping hands, which are actually steam hammers – perhaps a young visitor to the gallery would then hurry down the long stairway, past all the tiers, dash into the ring, shout Stop! through the fanfares of the constantly modulating orchestra.

But since it is not like this; a beautiful woman, white and red, glides in through the curtains, which the proud ushers part for her; the ringmaster, devotedly trying to catch her eye, breathes at her crouching like an animal; carefully lifts her onto the dappled grey as if she were his beloved granddaughter about to embark on a dangerous journey; cannot decide to give the signal with his whip; finally, with a tremendous effort, cracks it with a bang; runs open-mouthed beside the horse; follows with a keen eye the equestrienne's leaps; can scarcely comprehend her artistry;

attempts to alert her by shouting in English; angrily exhorts the grooms holding the hoops to be totally attentive; before the grand Salto Mortale implores the orchestra with raised hands that it should fall silent; finally lifts the girl from the trembling horse, kisses her on both cheeks and considers no ovation from the public sufficient; while she herself, leaning on him for support, standing on tiptoe in a cloud of dust, with outstretched arms, reclined head, wants to share her happiness with the entire circus – since it is so, the gallery visitor lays his face on the balustrade and, sinking into the final march as into a heavy dream, weeps without knowing it.

An Old Document

It is as if much has been neglected in the defence of our Fatherland. Until now, we haven't bothered about it and have just gone about our work; but recent events have given us cause for worry.

I have a cobbler's workshop in the square in front of the Imperial Palace. I have scarcely opened my shop at dawn before I see armed men occupying all the entrances to the streets leading to the square. However, they are not our soldiers, but apparently nomads from the north. In a manner that I cannot comprehend, they have driven all the way to the capital, although it is far from the border. In any case, they are here; it appears that every morning there are more of them.

In accordance with their nature, they camp in the open, because they detest houses. They busy themselves with honing their swords and sharpening their arrows, and drilling on horseback. They have literally made a stable out of this tranquil, scrupulously clean square. Although we sometimes run out of our shops and try to get rid of at least the worst of the filth, it occurs less and less frequently, because the effort is futile and, moreover, exposes us to the danger of being trampled by the wild horses or being injured by a whip.

You cannot speak with the nomads. They don't know our language, in fact they hardly

have one of their own. Among themselves, they communicate like jackdaws. Again and again, you hear this screeching of the jackdaw. Our way of life and our institutions are as incomprehensible to them as they are insignificant. As a result, they also reject every attempt to use sign language. You can dislocate your jaw and twist your hands out of joint, and still they haven't understood you and will never understand you. They often make grimaces; then the whites of their eyes spin around and foam spills from their mouths, though they neither mean to say anything nor frighten anyone with this; they do it because it is their way. What they need, they take. You cannot say that they use violence. Before they act, you step aside and let them have everything.

They have also taken some good pieces from my stock. But I cannot complain when I see, for example, how it is for the butcher across the street. Hardly has he brought in his wares than everything has been snatched away and is being devoured by the nomads. Their horses eat meat too; often, horse and rider lie side by side and feed on the same piece of meat, each at one end. The butcher is afraid and doesn't dare to call off the meat deliveries. We understand this, however, pool our money, and support him. Who knows what the nomads would think of doing if they got no meat; but who knows what they will think of doing even if they get meat every day.

Recently, the butcher thought that he could at least save himself the trouble of slaughtering, and brought a live ox in the morning. He must not do that again. I lay for a good hour flat on the floor right at the back of my shop, with all my clothes, blankets and pillows piled on top of me, just so I wouldn't have to hear the bellowing of the ox, which the nomads had attacked from all sides to tear pieces out of its warm flesh with their teeth. It was quiet for a long time before I had the nerve to venture out; the nomads lay spent around the ox's remains, like drinkers around a wine barrel.

Just at that time I thought I saw the Emperor himself through one of the windows of the palace; otherwise he never comes into these outer chambers, always lives exclusively in the innermost garden; this time, however, he stood, or so at least it seemed to me, at one of the windows and gazed with bowed head at the goings-on in front of his castle.

"How will it end up?" we ask ourselves. "How long will we put up with this burden and torment? The Imperial Palace attracted the nomads, but it does not know how to drive them away. The gate remains shut; the sentries, who used to march in and out ceremoniously, remain behind barred windows. The salvation of the Fatherland is in the hands of us craftsmen and merchants; but we are not up to such a task, never even claimed to be up to it. It's a misunderstanding, and it will be our ruin."

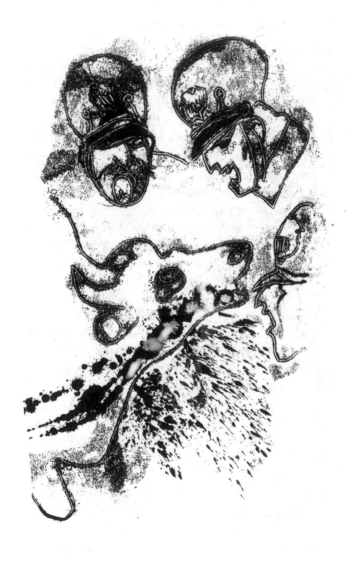

BEFORE THE LAW

Before the law stands a doorkeeper. A man from the country comes to this doorkeeper and requests admission to the law. But the doorkeeper says that he cannot grant him admission now. The man reflects and then asks if he will be allowed to enter later. "It is possible," the doorkeeper says, "but not now." Since the door to the law stands open, as always, and the doorkeeper steps aside, the man bends over to look through the doorway into the interior. When the doorkeeper notices this, he laughs and says: "If it tempts you so much, why don't you try to go in, despite my forbidding it. But take note: I am powerful. And I am only the lowliest doorkeeper. But from hall to hall other doorkeepers are posted, one more powerful than the other. Even I cannot bear the mere sight of the third one." The man from the country had not expected such difficulties; the law should always be accessible to everyone, he thinks, but as he now more closely observes the doorkeeper in his fur coat, with his big, sharp nose, the long, thin, black Tatar beard, he nevertheless decides that he would rather wait until he receives permission to enter. The doorkeeper gives him a stool and lets him sit beside the door. There he sits for days and years. He makes many attempts to get permission to enter, and tires the doorkeeper with his requests. The doorkeeper often holds brief interviews with him, interrogates him about his home and many other things, but they are disinterested questions, the kind great lords ask, and in the end he always tells him that he still cannot let him enter. The man, who has brought many provisions for his journey, uses everything, no matter how valuable, to bribe the doorkeeper. Although the doorkeeper accepts everything, he always says: "I am only accepting it so that you do not think you have neglected anything." Over the many years, the man observes the doorkeeper almost continuously. He forgets the other doorkeepers, and this first one appears to him as the only obstacle to his admission to the Law. He curses his bad fortune, in the early years loudly and without restraint; later, as he grows older, he merely grumbles to himself. He becomes childish and, since during his many years of observing the doorkeeper he has also come to know the fleas in his fur collar, he also begs the fleas to help him change the doorkeeper's mind. Finally, his vision begins to grow weak, and he does not know if it is actually getting darker or if it is only his eyes deceiving him. But now he can make out a glow that comes inextinguishably from the doorway of the Law. He does not have long to live now. Before his death, all of his experiences from this entire time accumulate in his head to form one question which he has not yet asked the doorkeeper. He beckons to him, since he can no longer raise his stiffening body. The doorkeeper has to bend very low, since the height difference between the two has changed, much to the man's disadvantage. "What else do you still want to know?" asks the doorkeeper. "You're insatiable." "Everyone strives for the Law," says the man. "How is it that, in all these years, no one except me has sought admission to the Law?" The doorkeeper realizes that the man has reached his end, and to get through to him despite his growing deafness, he shouts at him: "No one else could have gained admission here, because this entrance was intended only for you. Now I will go and shut it."

JACKALS AND ARABS

We camped at the oasis. My companions were asleep. An Arab, tall and white, passed me; he had fed the camels and was going to his sleeping-place.

I threw myself backward onto the grass; I wanted to sleep; I could not; the plaintive howling of a jackal in the distance; I sat up again. And what was so far away was suddenly near. A teeming pack of jackals around me; their eyes gleamed a dull gold and faded again; lean bodies which moved swiftly and according to natural law, as if under the whip.

One of them came up behind me, squeezed itself through under my arm, tight against me as if it needed my warmth, then stood before me and spoke to me, almost eye to eye:

"I am the oldest jackal far and wide. I'm happy to still be able to greet you here. I'd almost given up hope because we've waited an eternity for you; my mother waited, and her mother, and all their mothers up to the mother of all jackals. Believe me!"

"That surprises me," I said, and forgot to kindle the pile of wood that had been prepared to keep away the jackals with its smoke. "It surprises me a great deal to hear it. I've come by sheer coincidence from the far north, and I am here on a short trip. What do you want, then, jackals?"

And as if encouraged by these perhaps far too friendly words, they moved in a tighter circle around me; all of them were panting and snarling.

"We know", began the oldest jackal, "that you come from the north, it's precisely on this that we have based our hope. There, in the north, is an intelligence that cannot be found here among the Arabs. You know, you can't strike a spark of intelligence from their cold arrogance. They kill animals to eat them, and they scorn carrion."

"Don't talk so loud," I said. "Arabs are sleeping nearby."

"You really are a stranger," the jackal said, "otherwise you would know that never in the history of the world has a jackal been afraid of an Arab. Why should we be afraid of them? Isn't it unfortunate enough that we've been cast out to live among such people?"

"Could be, could be," I said, "I don't make judgements on things that are so far beyond me; it seems to be a very old quarrel; it's probably in the blood; maybe it won't end with the blood."

"You're very clever," the old jackal said, and all of them panted more quickly, their lungs racing though they were standing still; a bitter odour, which at times could only be endured with clenched teeth, streamed out of their open snouts. "You're very clever; what you say corresponds to our ancient lore. So we just take their blood, and the quarrel is over."

"Oh!" I said, more fiercely than I had intended, "they will defend themselves; they'll shoot you down by the dozens with their muskets."

"You misunderstand us," he said, "as humans do, apparently even in the north. We're not going to kill them. There isn't enough water in the Nile to cleanse us of that. Why, we flee at the mere sight of their living bodies, to cleaner air, into the desert, which is our home for that reason."

And all the jackals on every side, which now included many newcomers from far away, sank their heads between their forelegs and cleaned them with their paws; it was as if they wanted to conceal a distaste so appalling that I wanted to escape out of their circle with one great leap.

"What do you intend to do?" I asked, and tried to stand; but I couldn't; two young animals had sunk their teeth into my coat and shirt; I had to remain seated. "They are holding your train," explained the old jackal earnestly, "a mark of honour." "They are to let go of me!" I shouted, turning now to the old jackal, now to the young. "Of course they will," the old one said, "if you want them to. But it will take a little time, because they have bitten deeply, as is the custom, and must open their jaws slowly. In the meantime, please listen to our request." "Your behaviour has, of course, not made me very receptive to it," I said. "Don't hold our clumsiness against us," he said and used for the first time the plaintive tone of his natural voice, "we are poor creatures, we only possess our teeth; for everything that we want to do, the good and the bad, we have nothing but our teeth." "So, what do you want?" I asked, little soothed.

"Sir," he cried, and all the jackals began to howl; it seemed to me, very remotely, to be a melody. "Sir, you must put an end to the quarrel that divides the world in two. You resemble so much the one our ancestors described who would accomplish this. We must be left in peace by the Arabs; breathable air; our view of the horizon purged of them; no bleating of the sheep slaughtered by the Arab; all animals are to die peacefully; we should be able to drain the carcass of its blood and clean its bones without being disturbed. We want cleanliness, nothing but cleanliness" – and now they all wept and sobbed – "how can you endure living in this world, O noble heart and sweet entrails? Dirt is their white; dirt is their black; their beards are a horror; just a glimpse of the corners of their eyes makes you want to spit; and when they raise their arms, all hell breaks loose in their armpits. And so, sir, and so, O dear sir, with the aid of your all-capable hands, with the aid of your all-capable hands cut their throats with these scissors!" And in response to a jerk of his head, a jackal aproached carrying in his eye tooth a small pair of sewing scissors covered with old rust.

"Ah, the scissors at last, and now no more!" cried the Arab leader of our caravan, who had sneaked up to us from downwind and now cracked his great whip.

The jackals fled in geat haste, but they remained huddled together at some distance, the many beasts so tightly pressed together and rigid that they resembled a small wattled fence encircled by will-o'-the-wisps.

"So you too, sir, have seen and heard this spectacle," the Arab said, and laughed as jovially as the reticence of his race permitted. "So you know what the animals want?" I asked. "Of course, sir," he said, "but everybody knows that; for as long as there have been Arabs, these scissors have wandered through the desert, and they will wander with us for all time. They are offered to every European for the great task; every European is the very person predestined for the jackals. These animals possess a ridiculous hope; they are fools, real fools. That's why we love them; they are our dogs; more beautiful than your own. Just look, a camel died during the night, I've had it brought here."

Four bearers came and threw the heavy carcass down in front of us. It had scarcely touched the ground before the jackals raised their voices. As if each and every one of them were pulled irresistibly by a rope, they approached, hesitantly, their bodies grazing the ground. They had forgotten the Arabs, forgotten the hatred; the all-obliterating presence of the cadaver's stench bewitched them. One was already at the throat, and its first bite found the artery. Like a small frenetic pump working unconditionally and hopelessly to extinguish an uncontrollable fire, every muscle in its body tugged and twitched in its place. And now they all piled on the carcass and, heaped high as a mountain, were working at the same chore.

The caravan leader now fiercely lashed them all over with his stinging whip. They raised their heads; half in an intoxicated trance; they saw the Arabs standing before them; now felt the sting of the whip on their snouts; retreated in a bound and ran back some way. But the camel's blood already lay there in steaming pools; the carcass was torn wide open in many places. They could not resist it; they were back again; again the caravan leader lifted his whip; I gripped his arm.

"You are right, sir," he said, "we will let them do their job; it is also time to set off. You've seen them. Marvellous creatures, aren't they? And how they despise us!"

A Visit to a Mine

Today, the chief engineers came down to visit us. Management has issued some orders to bore new galleries, and so the engineers came to take the first measurements. How young these people are and still so dissimilar! They have all developed in freedom, and already at their young ages their clearly distinguished characters have revealed themselves independently.

One of them, with black hair, animated, takes in everything with his eyes.

A second, with a notebook, makes jottings as he walks, looks about, compares, notes down.

A third, with his hands in his coat pockets so that everything about him is tense, walks erect; maintains his dignity; only the constant biting of his lips reveals his impatient, irrepressible youth.

A fourth provides explanations to the third, who has not asked for them; smaller than the latter, running next to him like a tempter, his index finger always in the air, he appears to be holding a litany on everything that can be seen here.

A fifth, perhaps the highest in rank, tolerates no escorts; now he is in front, now behind; the group accommodates its pace to his; he is pale and weak; responsibility has drained his eyes; often, while reflecting, he presses his hand to his forehead.

The sixth and seventh walk somewhat bent over, their heads close together, arm in arm, exchanging confidences; if our coal mine and our workplace weren't obviously here in the deepest gallery, one might think that these bony, clean-shaven, bulbous-nosed gentlemen were young clergymen. One of them laughs mostly to himself with catlike purrs; the other, also laughing, does most of the talking and keeps some kind of beat with his free hand. How certain these two men must be of their jobs; yes, what services they must already have rendered to our mine despite their youth to be allowed to busy themselves so unwaveringly only with their own affairs or at least with matters not connected to the task at hand, right under the nose of their boss, at such an important inspection. Or is it possible that, despite all their laughter and inattentiveness, they do notice what they need to? One hardly dares to make a definitive judgement about men like these.

On the other hand, however, there is no doubt that, for example, the eighth is incomparably more attentive than these two, in fact more than any of the other men. He has to touch everything and rap it with a small hammer that he keeps pulling out of a pocket and putting back again. Sometimes, despite being elegantly dressed, he kneels down in the dirt and raps the ground, and then again, while walking along, raps the walls or the ceiling above his head. Once he stretched himself at full length along the ground and lay still; we thought that something had happened to him; but then, with a twitch of his trim body, he sprang to his feet. He had merely performed another examination. We believe that we know our mine and its rocks, but we cannot understand what this engineer keeps examining here in this manner.

A ninth pushes before him a kind of perambulator containing the measuring instruments. Very expensive devices deeply embedded in the softest cotton. Actually, the porter should have been pushing this carriage, but he is not trusted to do it; an engineer had to be used, and he does it gladly, as one can see. He is probably the youngest; perhaps he does not yet understand all the instruments, but his glance often falls on them; as a result, he almost risks running into the wall with the perambulator now and then.

But there is another engineer who walks along beside the perambulator and prevents that from happening. Apparently, this one understands the instruments inside-out and seems to be their real guardian. From time to time, without stopping the perambulator, he takes a part out, examines it, screws it open or shut, shakes and taps it, holds it against his ear and listens; and finally, mostly when the driver has stopped, lays the small thing, which is almost invisible from a distance, very carefully back in the wagon. This engineer is a bit domineering, but only on behalf of the

instruments. Ten steps in front of the vehicle, we are supposed to make way for it at a silent finger signal, even where there is no room to make way for it.

The idle porter walks behind these two gentlemen. The gentlemen, as is only natural given their great knowledge, have divested themselves of all arrogance, the porter, on the other hand, appears to have accumulated it in himself. With one hand on his back, the other in front over his gilt buttons or caressing the fine cloth of his uniform jacket, he often nods right and left, as if he assumed that we had saluted him but could not, from his exalted height, be certain of it. Of course, we do not salute him, but at the sight of him, you might almost think that it is something tremendous to be an office porter for the mine's board of directors. However, we laugh at him behind his back, but since even a thunderclap could not make him turn around, he remains something incomprehensible that we respect.

Today there will not be much more work done; the interruption was too great; a visit like that takes away all thoughts about work. It is all too tempting to watch the gentlemen in the darkness of the trial gallery in which they have all disappeared. And our shift is almost over; we will not see the gentlemen return.

THE NEXT VILLAGE

My grandfather used to say: "Life is astonish-
ingly short. Now, in my memory, it is so com-
pressed that I can hardly understand, for example, how a young person can decide to ride
to the next village without being afraid that
– apart from accidents – even the time allotted
to a normal, happy life is far too short for such
a journey."

AN IMPERIAL MESSAGE

The Emperor – so the story goes – has sent a message to you, the individual, the miserable subject, the tiny shadow who has fled the imperial sun to the remotest point, to you of all people the Emperor has sent a message from his deathbed. He made the messenger kneel at his bedside and whispered the message in his ear; so important was it to him that he made the messenger repeat it in a whisper. He then confirmed its accuracy with a nod of his head. And in front of all the spectators of his death – all obstructing walls are being torn down and on the broad stairways sweeping upwards the Empire's great and mighty stand in a circle – in front of all of these he dispatched the messenger. The messenger immediately set out on the journey; a powerful, an indefatigable man; thrusting one arm forward, then the other, he makes his way through the crowd; if he encounters resistance, he points to the sign of the sun on his breast; he advances easily, as no one else could. But the crowd is so great; there is no end to their dwellings. If he came to open fields, how he would fly, and you would soon hear the wonderful beating of his fists upon your door. But how fruitlessly he struggles instead; he is still squeezing through the chambers of the innermost palace; he will never get through them; and if he did succeed in this, he would have gained nothing; he would have to fight his way down the stairs; and if he did succeed in that, he would have gained nothing; the courtyards would have to be crossed; and after the courtyards, the second outer palace; and again stairs and courtyards; and again a palace; and so on for thousands of years; and if he finally burst through the outermost gate – but this can never, never happen – the imperial capital would lie before him, the centre of the world piled high with its dregs. No one makes it through here, not even with a message from a dead man. But you sit at your window and dream of it when evening comes.

THE CONCERN OF THE HEAD
OF A FAMILY

Some say that the word Odradek comes from
the Slavic and attempt to demonstrate the formation of the word on this basis. Others believe that it comes from the German and is
only influenced by the Slavic. The uncertainty
of both interpretations, however, allows us to
conclude, justifiably, that neither applies, especially since neither helps us find a meaning
for the word.

Of course, no one would occupy himself
with such studies if there actually did not exist
a being named Odradek. At first, it resembles
a flat, star-shaped spool for thread, and it
does indeed seem to be wrapped with thread;
however, it is probably only old, torn-off bits
of thread, knotted together and tangled, of the
most varied types and colours. However, it is
not only a spool, but a small crossbar sticks
out of the centre of the star, and another one
is attached to this one at a right angle. With
the aid of this last rod and one of the points
of the star on the other side, the whole thing
can stand erect as if on two legs.

It is tempting to believe that this figure once
had some functional shape and that it is now
only a broken remnant. This does not, however, seem to be the case; at least, there is no
indication of that; there are no joints or cracks
to be seen anywhere that would suggest

anything of the kind; the whole thing seems senseless, yet also complete in a way. In any case, more cannot be said about it, since Odradek is extremely agile and impossible to catch.

He spends his time alternately in the attic, on the stairs, in the corridors and in the hall. Sometimes he cannot be seen for months; probably because he has moved to other houses; but inevitably he always returns to our house. Sometimes, when you have just stepped through the door and he is downstairs leaning against the banisters, you feel like speaking to him. Naturally, you don't ask him difficult questions, but treat him – his diminutive size alone encourages you to do so – like a child. "So, what's your name?" you ask him. "Odradek," he says. "And where do you live?" "Indefinite residence," he says and laughs; but it is laughter that can only be produced without lungs. It sounds a bit like the rustling of fallen leaves. That is usually the end of the conversation. In any case, even these answers sometimes fail to materialize; he often remains silent for a long time, like the piece of wood he appears to be.

I ask myself, in vain, what will happen to him. Can he die? Everything that dies has a kind of objective, a kind of activity, and has ground itself down at it; but this does not apply to Odradek. Is he, then, supposed to roll down the stairs in days to come, trailing bits of thread, at the feet of my children and my children's children? Apparently, he is hurting no one; but the thought that he will outlive me I find almost painful.

ELEVEN SONS

I have eleven sons.

The first is outwardly very unattractive, but serious and clever; although I love him him as I love all my children, I do not think very highly of him. His thinking strikes me as too simple. He looks neither to the right nor to the left and not into the distance either; with the limited scope of his thoughts, he is always running around or, rather, spinning.

The second is handsome, slim, well built; it is a delight to watch him in the fencing stance. He too is clever, but worldly-wise as well; he has seen much, and this is why even our nature here at home seems to open itself to him more than to the stay-at-home. But it is certain that he owes this advantage not only, and not even essentially, to his travels, it is much more a trait of this child's singular personality, which is, for example, recognized by anyone who wants to imitate, say, his high dive into the water in which he somersaults several times and still manages to maintain a vigorous self-control. The imitator's courage holds out until the end of the diving board, where instead of diving he sits down abruptly and raises his arms in apology. – But despite all this (I should actually be happy to have such a child), my relationship with him is not untroubled. His left eye is a little smaller than his right and blinks a lot; a small flaw, certainly, that makes his face even more audacious than it would otherwise be, and given the unapproachable inwardness of his character no one would criticize this smaller, blinking eye. I, the father, do so. Of course, it is not this physical flaw that pains me, but a small irregularity in his spirit that somehow corresponds to it, some poison coursing through his blood, some inability, a tendency which only I can see and prevents him from perfecting his life. This is, however, precisely what makes him my true son, because this flaw is also the flaw of our entire family and only too apparent in this son.

The third son is just as handsome, but it is a beauty that I do not like. He has the good looks of a singer: the curving mouth; the dreamy eye; the head that requires drapery behind it to create an effect; the excessively arching chest; the hands that readily fly up and much too readily drop; the legs that hesitate because they cannot support his weight. And furthermore: the tone of his voice is not full; it fools you for a moment; those in the know prick up their ears; but it soon runs out of breath. – Although, generally, everything tempts me to put this son on show, I prefer to keep him hidden; he himself doesn't force himself on anyone, but not because he is aware of his failings, rather out of naivety. Also, he feels like a stranger in our time; as if he were a member of our family as well as another one that is forever lost to him, he is often listless and nothing can cheer him up.

My fourth son is perhaps the friendliest of them all. A true child of his time, he can be understood by anyone, he stands on ground common to all and everyone feels like nodding to him. Perhaps this universal acknowledgement lends lightness to his character, freedom to his movements, nonchalance to his judgements. Some of his remarks are worth repeating, but only some, because all in all he is afflicted with just too much nonchalance. He is like someone who admirably dives, cleaves the air like a swallow, but still ends up hopelessly in barren dust, a nothing. Thoughts like these spoil the sight of this child for me.

The fifth son is kind and good; promised much less than he delivered; was so insignificant that you really felt alone in his presence; but has achieved a certain standing. If you asked me how that happened, I could hardly come up with an answer. Perhaps it is easiest for innocence to pass through the raging elements in this world, and he is innocent. Perhaps too innocent. Friendly to everyone. Perhaps too friendly. I admit: I don't feel good when someone praises him to me. After all, it means you are giving praise a bit too easily if you praise someone as obviously praiseworthy as my son. My sixth son seems, at least at first glance, the most profound of them all. Loves to hang his head, and yet a chatterbox. This is why you don't easily get the better of him. If he's about to lose, he sinks into invincible melancholy; if he gets the advantage, he maintains it through chattering. But I won't deny that he possesses a certain oblivious passion; in daylight, he often fights his way through his thoughts as in a dream. Without falling ill – on the contrary, his health is very good – he staggers sometimes, especially in the twilight, but he requires no help, he doesn't fall. Perhaps his physical development is to blame for this phenomenon, he is much too tall for his age. This makes him ugly all in all, despite strikingly beautiful particulars, his hands and feet, for example. Incidentally, his forehead is also ugly; somehow shrivelled in both its skin and its bone formation

The seventh son belongs to me perhaps more than any of the others. The world does not know how to appreciate him; it does not understand his special kind of wit. I do not overrate him; I know that he is insignificant enough; if the world had no other flaw than that it cannot appreciate him enough, it would still be immaculate. But within the family, I would not want to be without this son. He contributes both disquiet and awe for tradition, and combines them, at least that's how I feel, into an indisputable whole. However, he himself knows least of all what to do with this whole; he will not start the wheel of the future rolling; but this tendency of his is so encouraging, so promising; I wish that he had children and they also had children. Unfortunately, this wish will apparently not be fulfilled. With a self-satisfaction that I can understand as much as I dislike, and which stands in splendid contradiction to the judgement of his environment, he goes around alone; doesn't care about girls and, despite this, will never lose his good humour.

My eighth son is my problem child, and I really don't know why. He looks strangely at me, although I feel close paternal ties to him. Time has made much good; earlier, however, I was sometimes seized by a trembling when I so much as thought about him. He goes his own way; has cut all ties to me; and will certainly, with his hard head, his small athletic body – only his legs were really weak when he was a boy, but that may have changed in the meantime – make it wherever he wants. Often, I feel like calling him back, asking him how he is doing, why he has cut himself off from his father and what it is he basically wants to do, but now he is so far away and so much time has passed, it may as well stay the way it is. I hear that he is the only one of my sons to sport a full beard; of course, that is not attractive on such a small man.

My ninth son is very elegant and possesses a honeyed glance meant for women. So honeyed that on occasion he can seduce even me, although I know that literally a wet sponge is enough to wipe away the heavenly radiance. Special about this boy is that he does not try to be seductive at all; it would suffice him to lie upon a sofa for his whole life and squander his gaze on the ceiling or, better still, be allowed to keep it beneath his eye-lids. When he is in this favourite position of his, then he is happy to talk and talks quite well; succinctly and vividly; however, only within narrow limits; if he goes beyond them, which is impossible to avoid since they are so narrow, his talk becomes wholly vacuous. You'd signal him to stop if there were any hope that his slumbering eyes could notice it.

My tenth son is taken for an insincere char-acter. I don't want to wholly refute or wholly confirm this flaw. It is certain that anyone who sees him coming with the solemnity of a man twice his age, with his frock coat always but-toned, in an old but meticulously brushed black hat, with his immobile face, the some-what jutting chin, the eyelids that bulge out over his eyes, two fingers sometimes at his mouth – anyone who sees him like this will think: this is an out-and-out hypocrite. But just listen to him speak! Sensibly; circumspectly; brusquely; foiling questions with mischievous zeal; in astonishing, self-evident, and cheerful accord with the universe; an accord which, of necessity, straightens the neck and lifts the head. Many who consider themselves very clever and for this reason, as they believed, were repelled by his appearance, have be-come strongly attracted to him because of his words. However, there are also people who are indifferent to his appearance but regard his words as hypocritical. I, as his father, do not want to decide here, but I must admit, in

any case, that the latter critics are more note-worthy than the former.

My eleventh son is delicate, probably the weakest of all my sons; but his weakness is deceptive; for he can at times be strong and resolute, but even then the weakness is some-how at the bottom of it. But it is no shame-ful weakness, rather something that seems like a weakness on this earth of ours. For instance, is not readiness for flight also a weakness, since it is hesitation and uncertainty and flut-tering? My son exhibits something like that. Of course, these are not characteristics that delight a father; indeed, they are evidently meant to destroy the family. Sometimes he looks at me as if he wants to say: "I will take you with me, Father." Then I think: "You'd be the last I would entrust myself to." And again his look appears to say: "Then let me be at least the last."

Those are my eleven sons.

A Fratricide

It has been proven that the murder was committed as follows:

At about 9 o'clock on a moonlit evening, Schmar, the murderer, positioned himself on the street corner where Wese, the victim, had to turn off the street where his office was located and into the street in which he lived.

The night air was so cold it froze the blood. But Schmar had put on only a thin blue suit; and the jacket was unbuttoned. He did not feel the cold; in addition, he was in constant motion. He held his murder weapon, half bayonet, half kitchen knife, firmly and fully exposed. Examined the knife in the moonlight; the blade flashed; not sufficiently for Schmar; he slashed at the stones of the pavement with it until sparks flew; regretted it, perhaps; and, to undo the damage, drew it like the bow of a violin over the sole of his boot while he, standing on one leg, bent forward, listening to both the sound of the knife on his boot and the noise in the fateful side street.

Why did citizen Pallas, who not far away was observing this from his second-storey window, permit it to happen? Fathom human nature! With his collar turned up, his dressing gown secured around his stout body, he gazed down shaking his head.

And five houses down, on the opposite side of the street, Mrs Wese, wearing her fox fur

over her nightgown, looked out for her husband, who was lingering unusually long today.

Finally, the doorbell in front of Wese's office sounded, too loud for a doorbell, over the city, up to heaven, and Wese, the industrious night-worker, emerged from the building, still invisible in that street, announced only by the sound of the bell; immediately, the pavement chronicled his calm footsteps.

Pallas bends far foward; he must not miss a thing. Mrs Wese, soothed by the bell, shuts her window with a rattle. But Schmar kneels down; since no other part of his body is bare, he presses only his face and hands against the stones; where everything freezes, Schmar is red hot.

Precisely on the border separating the two streets, Wese comes to a halt, he leans into the other street only with his walking stick. A whim. The night sky has enticed him, the dark blue and the gold. Oblivious, he looks up at it, oblivious he strokes his hair beneath the hat he has doffed; nothing up there comes together to indicate to him his immediate future; everything remains in its senseless, unfathomable place. In and of itself, it is very sensible that Wese walks on, but he walks into Schmar's knife.

"Wese!" screams Schmar, standing on tiptoe, his arm raised, the knife sharply lowered; "Wese! Julia is waiting in vain!" And right into the throat and left into the throat and a third time deep into the belly stabs Schmar. Water

rats slit open make a sound like Wese is making now.

"Done," Schmar says and throws the knife, the superflous bloody ballast, against the front of the nearest house. "The bliss of murder! Relief, inspiration through the shedding of another's blood! Wese, old night-shade, friend, pub companion, you're oozing away into the dark soil beneath the street. Why aren't you just a blood-filled bladder so that I could sit on you and you would disappear completely. Not every wish is granted, not every blossoming dream bears fruit, your heavy remains lie here, already impervious to every kick. So what's the point of the mute question you ask in this way?"

Pallas, gagging indiscriminately on every poison in his body, stands in his double-winged house door as it flies open. "Schmar! Schmar! Saw it all, didn't miss a thing." Pallas and Schmar examine each other. The scrutiny pleases Pallas, Schmar doesn't know what to think.

With a throng of people on either side, Mrs Wese rushes to the scene, her face aged by terror. Her fur coat swings open, she falls over Wese, the nightgowned body belongs to him, the fur coat, which closes over the couple like the grass over a grave, belongs to the crowd.

Schmar, stifling with difficulty the last of his nausea, his mouth pressed against the shoulder of the policeman who, treading lightly, leads him away.

A Dream

Josef K. dreamed:

It was a lovely day and K. wanted to go for a walk. But hardly had he gone two steps when he was already at the cemetery. The paths there were very artificial and impractically twisted, but he glided along one hovering imperturbably, as if on a rushing torrent. While still far away, he was already eyeing a freshly shovelled grave mound at which he wanted to rest. This grave mound was almost a temptation for him, and he felt he could not reach it fast enough. Sometimes, however, he scarcely saw the grave mound, it was concealed by flags that twisted and flapped against each other with great force; the flag-bearers could not be seen, but there appeared to be a celebration in progress there.

While he was still looking off into the distance, he suddenly saw the very same grave mound beside him; why, it was almost already behind him. He quickly leaped onto the grass. Since the path beneath his take-off foot continued running on, he tottered and fell onto his knees right in front of the grave mound. Two men were standing behind the grave holding a gravestone in the air between them; scarcely had K. appeared when they pushed the stone into the earth and it stood there as if firmly cemented. Immediately a third man emerged from behind a bush, a man K. recognized at once as an artist. He wore only a pair of trousers and a badly buttoned shirt; he had a velvet cap on his head; in his hand he held an ordinary pencil with which he was already drawing figures in the air as he approached.

With this pencil he now applied himself to the top of the stone; the stone was very tall, he did not have to bend down at all, but he had to bend forward since the grave mound, upon which he did not want to step, separated him from the stone. So he stood on his toes and supported himself with his left hand pressed against the stone's flat surface. With particular dexterity, he managed to produce golden letters with the ordinary pencil; he wrote: "Here lies –" Each letter emerged distinct and beautifully formed, deeply carved and in pure gold. After he had written the two words, he looked back at K.; K., who was anxious to find out how the inscription would read, scarcely noticed the man, but instead looked only at the stone. And, in fact, the man applied himself again to the writing, but he could not continue, there was some obstacle, he let the pencil sink and turned again toward K. Now K. also looked at the artist and noticed that he was deeply embarrassed but was unable to say why. All his earlier energy had disappeared. As a result, K. also felt embarrassed; they exchanged helpless glances; there was some ghastly misunderstanding which neither of them could clear up. At just the wrong time, a bell from the cemetery chapel began to toll, but the artist gestured with his raised hand and it stopped. After a little while, it began again; this time very softly and, without any particular command, broke off again at once; it was as if it only wanted to test its sound. K. was inconsolable over the artist's situation, he began to weep and sobbed for a long time into his hands. The artist waited until K. calmed down, and then decided, since he found no other way out, to go on with his writing. The first small stroke he made was a release for K., but the artist evidently achieved it only with the greatest reluctance; also, the writing was no longer as beautiful, above all it seemed to be lacking in gold, the stroke stretched out pale and uncertain, the letter only became very big. It was a J, it was almost completed when the artist furiously stamped on the grave mound with his foot so that the dirt around it flew into the air. Finally K. understood him; there was no longer any time to apologize to him; with all his fingers he dug into the earth, which offered almost no resistance; everything seemed prepared; a thin earthen crust had been contrived only for the sake of appearance; directly beneath it a large hole with very steep sides opened up into which K. sank, turned onto his back by a gentle current. And as he was already being received by the impenetrable depth, his head still set straight upon his neck, his name swept across the stone with great flourishes.

Delighted by this sight, he awoke.

A REPORT FOR AN ACADEMY

Esteemed gentlemen of the Academy!

You have paid me the honour of inviting me to submit to the Academy a report about my former life as an ape.

Unfortunately, I am unable to grant the request in the sense it was made. Almost five years separate me from apehood, a short time, perhaps, when measured by the calendar, but infinitely long to gallop through as I have done, accompanied here and there by splendid people, advice, applause, and orchestral music, but basically alone, because all my escorts, to maintain the metaphor, stayed well away from the jumps. This achievement would have been impossible if I had obstinately wanted to cling to my origins, to the memories of my youth. In fact, forsaking all obstinacy was the supreme commandment that I imposed on myself; I, a free ape, submitted myself to this yoke. As a result, however, my memories shut themselves off from me more and more. If, at the beginning, I could have returned, had the humans allowed it, through the gateway formed by the heaven above the earth, that opening grew lower and narrower as I was whipped on in my development; I felt better in the human world and more a part of it; the storm that blew at me out of my past grew calm; today it is merely a draught that cools my heels; and the distant hole through which it comes and through which I once came has grown so small that, even if I did have the strength and the will to run all the way back to it, I would have to flay the fur from my body to pass through it. Frankly, as much as I like to use images for these things, frankly speaking: your apehood, gentlemen, to the extent that you have something of the kind in your past, cannot be more remote from you than mine is from me. But everyone who walks the earth has heels that itch: the small chimpanzee and the great Achilles.

But perhaps I can answer your question in the narrowest sense, and I even do so with the greatest pleasure. The first thing I learned was: to give a handshake; a handshake indicates candour; may today, as I stand at the acme of my career, the candid word be added to that first handshake. It will not contribute anything essentially new to the Academy and will fall far short of what has been asked of me and what I, with the best will in the world, am unable to say – nevertheless, it should demonstrate the principle by which a former ape entered the human world and established himself there. But I would certainly not be able to say the trifle that follows if I were not completely sure of myself and my position on the stages of the great music halls of the world had not been secured to the point of being unshakeable:

I come from the Gold Coast. On how I was captured I have to rely on the reports of others.

A hunting expedition by the Hagenbeck Company – by the way, I've drained many a bottle of good red wine with its leader since then – was lying in wait in the bushes on a riverbank when I came to drink there with a troop of apes. Shots were fired; I was the only one who was hit; I received two wounds.

One in the cheek; that one was slight; but it left a large bare red scar that earned me the revolting and totally inappropriate name of Red Peter, which could only have been made up by an ape, as if the only difference between me and the performing ape Peter, who croaked not long ago and was known here and there, was the red spot on my cheek. This only in passing.

The second shot struck me below the hip. This was a serious wound, it is the reason that I still limp a little today. Recently I read in an article by one of the ten thousand windbags who air their opinions about me in the papers: my ape nature has not yet been completely repressed; the proof of this is that when visitors come to see me I am particularly fond of removing my trousers to show where that shot went in. Every finger of that fellow's writing hand should be shot off one by one. As for me, I can take off my trousers in front of whomever I want; you won't find anything there but well-groomed fur and the scar from a – here let us choose a specific word for a specific purpose, not to be misunderstood, however – the scar from a wanton shot.

Everything is out in the open; there's nothing to hide; when it comes to the truth, all the great minds throw refinement to the winds. If, on the other hand, the aforementioned writer were to take off his trousers when visitors come, that would be something else and I view it as a sign of his good sense that he does not do it. But then let him leave me alone with his tactfulness.

After these shots I awoke – and here, gradually, begin my own recollections – in a cage in the steerage of the Hagenbeck steamer. It was not a cage with bars on all sides; instead, only three sides were attached to a crate; the crate therefore formed the fourth side. The whole thing was too low to stand upright in and too narrow to sit down in. So I squatted with my knees bent and constantly trembling, and also, since at the beginning I probably did not want to see anyone and wanted always to stay in the dark, I faced the crate while the bars of the cage cut into my hind flesh. This method of confining wild animals during the very first days of captivity is considered advantageous, and today I cannot deny, based on my experience, that from the human standpoint this really is the case.

But at the time I did not think about that. For the first time in my life I had no way out; straight ahead, at least, would not do; straight ahead in front of me was the crate, board fixed solidly to board. Although a continuous gap ran between the boards, which when I first discovered it I greeted with a rapturous howl of ignorance, this gap was not even anywhere near wide enough to stick my tail through and not all the strength of an ape could enlarge it.

As I was later told, I apparently made unusually little noise, from which it was assumed that either I would soon die or, if I survived the first critical period, I would be very easy to train. I survived this period. Glumly sobbing, painfully searching for fleas, wearily licking a coconut, knocking my skull against the wall of the crate, sticking out my tongue when anyone came near me – these were my first pursuits in my new life. But in all of it only the one feeling: no way out. Of course, what I felt then as an ape I can today only put into human words, and therefore I misrepresent it, but even if I can no longer attain the old ape truth, at least my description points in its direction, of that there is no doubt.

I'd had so many ways out before, and now I had none. I was stuck. If I had been nailed down, my freedom of movement would not have been any smaller. Why? You can scratch open the flesh between your toes and you won't find the reason. If you press your back against the bar of your cage until it almost cuts you in two, you won't find the reason. I had no way out, but I had to contrive one, because without it I could not live. Always against the side of this crate – I would inevitably have died. But at Hagenbeck apes belong against the side of a crate – well, so

I stopped being an ape. A clear, beautiful train of thought which I must somehow have cooked up with my belly, because apes think with the belly.

I am afraid that no one will understand just what I mean by a way out. I am using the expression in its fullest and most ordinary sense. I intentionally do not say freedom. I don't mean that grand feeling of freedom on all sides. Perhaps I knew it as an ape, and I have met humans who long for it. As far as I was concerned, however, I neither demanded freedom then nor do I demand it today. Incidentally: humans betray themselves all too often with freedom. And as freedom is counted as one of the most sublime feelings, so too is the corresponding delusion among the most sublime. In music halls I have often seen, before my entrance, some duo of artistes bustling about on the trapeze up near the ceiling. They vaulted, they swung, they sprang, they floated in each other's arms, one carried the other by the hair with his teeth. "This, too, is human freedom," I thought, "imperious movement." What a mockery of holy nature! No structure would withstand the laughter of the apes at such a sight.

No, freedom I did not want. Only a way out; right, left, it didn't matter which way; I made no other demands; even if the way turned out to be only an illusion; the demand was small, the delusion would not have been any bigger. To get somewhere, to get somewhere! Just not to stand still with raised arms, pressed against the side of a crate.

Today I can see it clearly: without the greatest inner composure I would never have been able to get away. And, in fact, I probably owe everything I have become to the composure that took hold of me after my first days on the ship. And, in turn, I owe this composure to the people on the ship.

They are good people, despite everything. Today I still recall with pleasure the sound of their heavy footsteps, which at the time echoed in my mind while I dozed. They were in the habit of doing everything as slowly as possible. If one of them wanted to rub his eyes, he lifted his hand as if it were a drooping weight. Their jokes were coarse, but sincere. Their laughter was always mixed with a dangerous-sounding but insignificant bark. In their mouths they always had something to spit out and they did not care where they spat it. They always complained that my fleas were jumping across onto them; but they were never truly angry at me for that; they well knew that fleas flourished in my fur and that fleas are jumpers; they reconciled themselves to it. When they were off duty, some of them occasionally sat around me in a semicircle; hardly spoke, only cooed at each other; smoked pipes while stretched out on crates; slapped their knees as soon as I made the slightest movement; and now and then one of them took a stick and tickled me where it

felt good. If I were invited today to take a cruise on this ship, I would certainly turn down the invitation, but it is just as certain that not all the memories I would recall there in the steerage would be repugnant.

The composure that I acquired in this circle of people kept me above all from attempting to escape. Viewed from today, it seems to me that I at least suspected that I would have to find a way out if I wanted to live, but that this way out was not to be achieved by escaping. I no longer know if escape was possible, but I believe that it was; escape should always be possible for an ape. With the teeth I have today I must be careful when just cracking nuts, but back then I would certainly have eventually succeeded in biting through the lock of my cage. I did not do it. What would I have gained by it? As soon as I stuck my head out, they would have caught me again and locked me in an even worse cage; or I could have slipped unnoticed among the other animals, among the giant snakes, say, across from me and breathed my last in their embrace; or I might have succeeded in stealing up to the deck and jumping overboard, then I would have rocked for a little while on the ocean and eventually drowned. Acts of desperation. I did not calculate in such a human way, but under the influence of my surroundings I behaved as if I had calculated.

I did not calculate, but I did observe at my leisure. I saw these people come and go, always the same faces, the same movements, often it seemed to me as if it were only one person. So, this person or these people came and went as they pleased. A lofty goal began to dawn on me. No one promised me that if I became like them, the bars of my cage would be removed. Such promises, for seemingly impossible conditions, are not made. But if you achieve the impossible, the promises appear after the fact precisely where you previously looked for them in vain. Now, there was nothing about these people that tempted me very much. Had I been an adherent of that freedom I have already described, I would certainly have preferred the ocean to the way out that presented itself in the dull glances of these people. In any case, I had been observing them for a long time before I thought about these things, indeed, it was the accumulated observations that first spurred me in this particular direction.

It was so easy to imitate these people. I could already spit in the first few days. Then we spat in each other's faces; the only difference was that I licked my face clean afterwards, and they didn't. I soon smoked a pipe like an old hand; if I then also pressed my thumb into the bowl of the pipe, the whole steerage let out a cheer; only it took me a long time to understand the difference between an empty pipe and a full one.

The schnapps bottle taxed me the most. The odour revolted me; I forced myself with all my strength; but weeks passed before I overcame my revulsion. The people took these internal struggles more seriously than anything else about me. I also do not differentiate among the people in my recollections, but there was one who always came, alone or with friends, by day, at night, at all hours; stood in front of me with the bottle and gave me lessons. He did not understand me, he wanted to solve the enigma of my being. He slowly uncorked the bottle and then looked at me, to check if I had understood; I admit that I always watched him with savage, unrestrained attention; no human teacher will ever find such a student of humankind on the face of the earth; after the bottle was uncorked, he lifted it to his lips; I follow it with my eyes all the way up to his throat; he nods, satisfied with me, and sets the bottle to his lips; I, delighted with my gradual enlightenment, scratch myself, screeching, from head to toe, wherever it needs scratching; he is pleased, tilts the bottle and takes a sip; I, impatient and desperate to imitate him, befoul myself in my cage, which also gives him great satisfaction; and now, holding the bottle at arm's length and bringing it up in one motion, he drains it in one swallow, bending backwards in an exaggerated manner to show me how it is done. I, exhausted from too much yearning, am unable to follow him any more and hang weakly on the bars of the cage, while he concludes his theoretical lesson by rubbing his belly and grinning.

Only now do the practical exercises begin. Am I not already too exhausted from the theory? Yes, much too exhausted. That is part of my destiny. Nevertheless, I reach, as best I can, for the proffered bottle; uncork it, trembling; success gradually fills me with renewed strength; I raise the bottle, now barely distinguishable from the original; set it to my lips and – and throw it with disgust, with disgust, although it is empty and filled only with the odour, throw it with disgust on the floor. To the sorrow of my teacher, to my own greater sorrow; I placate neither him nor myself by not forgetting, after I have thrown the bottle away, to rub my belly splendidly and grin.

All too often the lessons proceeded in this manner. And to my teacher's credit: he was not angry with me; true, he sometimes held the burning pipe against my fur until it began somewhere, where it was difficult for me to reach, to smoulder, but he then extinguished it himself with his enormous, benevolent hand; he was not angry with me, he understood that we were fighting on the same side against ape nature and that I had the more difficult job.

What a victory, then, it was for him and for me when, one evening in front of a large circle of onlookers – perhaps there was a party, a gramophone was playing, an officer strolled among the people – when on this evening, just when no one was looking, I picked up a schnapps bottle that had inadvertently been left in front of my cage, uncorked it exactly as I had been taught, as the assembled company began to watch me with growing attention, put it to my mouth and, without hesitating, without grimacing, like a professional drinker, with round rolling eyes, with gurgling throat, really and truly drank it empty; threw the bottle away no longer out of despair but as an artiste; forgot, however, to rub my belly; instead, because I couldn't do otherwise, because I was compelled, because my senses were reeling, called out a brief and distinct "Hello!", broke into human speech, with this shout sprang into human society and felt its echo, "Hey, listen, he's talking!", like a kiss upon my entire sweat-drenched body.

I repeat: I was not tempted to imitate human beings; I imitated them because I was looking for a way out, for no other reason. Also, this victory achieved little. My voice immediately failed me; returned only months later; my distaste for the schnapps bottle grew even stronger. But I had been given my direction once and for all.

When in Hamburg I was handed over to my first trainer, I soon recognized the two possibilities open to me: the zoo or the music hall. I did not hesitate. I said to myself: put all your energy into getting into the music hall; that is the way out; the zoo is only a new cage; if you are put there, you are lost.

And I learned, gentlemen. Oh, you learn when you have to; you learn when you want a way out; you learn at all costs. You supervise yourself with the whip; you mangle yourself at the slightest resistance. The ape nature fled head over heels out of me and away, so that, as a result, my first teacher almost became apelike himself and soon had to give up the lessons and was taken to a mental hospital. Fortunately, he was soon released.

But I used up many teachers, yes, even several teachers at once. As I grew more confident of my abilities, the public concerned itself with my progress and my future began to look bright, I engaged the teachers myself, had them sit in five adjoining rooms and learned from them all at the same time by leaping without pause from one room to the other.

This progress! This penetration from all sides of streams of knowledge into my awakening brain! I do not deny it: it delighted me. But I also admit: I did not overestimate it, not even then, how much less today. Through an effort that has until today not been equalled on the earth I have achieved the educational level of the average European. In and of itself that may be nothing at all, but it is something in that it helped me out of the cage and furnished me with this special way out, this human way out. There is an excellent German expression: sich in die Büsche schlagen, to slip away into the bushes; that's what I have done, I have slipped away into the bushes. I had no other choice, provided always that freedom was not an option.

If I look back at my development and its aim, I neither complain nor am I satisfied. With my hands in my trouser pockets, a bottle of wine on the table, I half lie and half sit in the rocking chair and gaze out of the window. If a visitor comes, I receive him as is fitting. My agent sits in the anteroom; when I ring, he comes and listens to what I have to say. Evenings there is almost always a performance, and my success can scarcely be greater. When I return home late at night from banquets, from scientific gatherings, from pleasant get-togethers, a small half-trained chimpanzee is waiting for me, and I amuse myself with her as apes do. By day I do not want to see her; she has, you see, the insane look of the half-trained animal in her eye; only I recognize it and I cannot bear it.

All in all, in any case, I have achieved what I wanted to achieve. You couldn't say it was not worth the effort. As for the rest, I am not looking for any human judgement, I only want to convey information, I am only reporting, to you as well, esteemed gentlemen of the Academy, I have only made a report.

"It is something very special to have a house of one's own."

Franz Kafka to his sister Ottla

Kafka's little house in the Golden Lane in the Prague Castle District.

Kafka in the Year 1916

A crisp, cold winter night in Prague, 1916. Up in the Golden Lane, a quiet corner of the Prague Castle District, a tall young man is stepping out of one of the tiny houses into the snow, carefully locking up by the dim light of a lantern and heading down the Old Castle Steps, descending into the sleeping city.

The man is the thirty-three-year-old Franz Kafka. By day, the doctor of law works for the Workers' Accident and Insurance Institute for the Kingdom of Bohemia, compiling reports and corresponding in German, and occasionally in Czech, with businessmen and the "most praiseworthy board of directors". In the evenings, he packs together a few small items in his room on the Lange Gasse (Czech: Dlouhá) and sets off through the narrow streets of the Prague Old Town, crosses the Vltava by the Manes Bridge, and climbs up to the little house in the Castle District to write. His works that have appeared to date, such as the anthology *Meditation* and the novellas *The Metamorphosis* and *In the Penal Colony*, are known only to a very narrow circle of readers. As recently as November, a reading in Munich had turned out to be a "magnificent failure".[1]

Left: The Golden Lane, *c.*1910.
Right: Franz Kafka at the age of 31.

However, in this winter of 1916 to 1917, Kafka is full of fresh spirit and it is at this time that he captures on paper most of the texts which will appear under the title *A Country Doctor: Short Stories* in 1920.[2]

The preceding months had been nowhere near as fruitful. Kafka had long been looking in vain for a quiet place to write. Concentrated work was impossible to imagine in his noisy room on the Dlouhá. "[I can hear] the sighs of my neighbours, the conversation of the residents downstairs, now and then a racket from the kitchen until well past 10 o'clock. Moreover, above the thin ceiling is the attic and the number of times that, in the late afternoon, just as I was about to start working on something, a maid hanging out the laundry has, quite innocently, trodden on my skull with her boot-heels, is incalculable. Now and then somebody also played the piano and, in the summer there was the sound of singing, a violin or a gramophone from the semicircle of the other encroaching houses. Therefore nothing approaching complete silence until after 11 o'clock at night. So the impossibility of attaining any peace, complete homelessness, breeding ground for all kinds of mania, ever greater weakness and forlornness."[3]

Ottilie Kafka, known as Ott-la, was the youngest of Kaf-ka's three sisters as well as the closest to him.

It was thanks to his sister Ottla, nine years his junior, that the author's search for accommodation was not in vain.

"Once in the summer I went with Ottla to look for an apartment, I no longer believed in the possibility of real peace but all the same I went to look. We looked at a few things in the Lesser Town, I was constantly thinking, if only there were a quiet hole somewhere in a corner of one of the old palaces, where one could finally stretch out in peace. Nothing, we found nothing actually. Just for fun, we enquired in the little alley. Yes, a house would be available for rent in November. Ottla, who is, in her way, also seeking peace, fell in love with the idea of renting the house [...]. It was lacking many things at first, I haven't the time to tell you how it has changed. Today it suits me perfectly. All in all: the way up there is lovely, it is quiet there, there is only a very thin wall separating me from my neighbour, but my neighbour is quiet enough; I carry my supper up there and am gener-ally there until midnight; then there are the advan-tages of walking home: I have to decide to stop but then I have the walk which cools my head."[4]

The House in the Golden Lane

Centuries before Kafka used the little house at number 22 as an isolated place to write, the humble buildings in the lane provided accommodation for lowly attendants at Prague Castle and simple craftsmen. It is probable that among them was a goldsmith or two, leading to the emergence of the name "Goldmakers' Lane". Under Emperor Rudolf II (1552–1612), the houses were used by a colourful band of residents – watchmen, castle marksmen, bellringers. Whether or not the legendary alchemists of Rudolf's time, who gave the lane the name "Alchemists' Lane", which is still in use today, lived among them, will probably remain a secret of history. Over the course of time, the narrow street has constantly changed its appearance: the houses have been restored, street lights have replaced the old paraffin lamps, and the muddy rivulet running down the middle of the lane has been channelled into

Inside Kafka's House

a conduit.[5] Thus, Kafka found a simple but enchanting place to write in a lane which is now filled with the noise of tourists: "It's something special to have one's own house, to shut out the world, not with the door just to the room or to the apartment, but the door to the whole building."[6]

View of Golden Lane, *c.*1940. The dark, squat house (fourth from the right) is number 22.

The Year 1916

The world which Kafka shut out with his door was a gloomy one: Europe was in the middle of the First World War. Kafka too had wanted to join up in the service of the Austrian army but, at the request of the Insurance Institute, he had been classified as "indispensable" and was therefore not released from work. Now, in the winter of 1916 to 1917, German soldiers and Allied troops were deadlocked in the West. The British Navy, which patrolled the seas of Europe, was cutting off its enemy's supply chain, and their stores were running ever lower. As priority was given to supplying the troops at the front, the cities were low on fuel and food. In addition to this, the news of the death of the Emperor Franz Joseph, who had also been King of Bohemia, reached Prague on 21st November. Now, after sixty-eight years and in the middle of a war, there was to be a change on the Habsburg throne. Great changes were also taking place in science and technology: The Bayerische Flugzeugwerke

Left: The First World War: Soldiers in the trenches.
Right: Emperor Franz Joseph

Left: It is possible that Albert Einstein encountered Kafka in Prague: In the years 1911 to 1912 he was teaching theoretical physics at the German university there.

Right: Felice and Franz in their engagement photo of 1917.

(Bavarian Aircraft Works) were established in March 1916 and a year later, they were renamed the Bayerische Motoren Werke (Bavarian Motor Works) – during the thirties, BMW rose to become a world-renowned motoring brand. In Russia, the longest stretch of railway track in the world, the Trans-Siberian Railway, was completed in October. From that year onwards, those interested in such matters could consult Albert Einstein's General Theory of Relativity and discover that even such lengthy railway tracks were only relative. However, progress of this sort did not help Ottla Kafka to obtain coal for the little house in the Golden Lane without great difficulty. Kafka was very well aware of the advantages of his tiny home in these circumstances.

"Yesterday, I overslept in the palace; when I made my way up to the little house, the fire was long since out and very cold […]. But then I took all the newspapers and even manuscripts and, after a while, achieved a quite lovely fire."[7]

It was not only the War and its consequences from which Kafka withdrew into his "monk's cell".[8] There were also difficulties in his private life. His relationship with his father was as strained as ever. Kafka even preferred to spend the evening of New

Year's Eve alone in the house in the Golden Lane. However, as his writing went well up there, this endowed him with a new sense of security and so he came to the decision to enter into a second engagement with Felice Bauer. They had broken off their first engagement in the summer of 1914 after only a few weeks. Kafka had no way of knowing that this second attempt at marriage would fail even before the end of 1917, or that he would be diagnosed with pulmonary tuberculosis, as he filled octavo exercise books with new stories in the winter of 1916 to 1917 up in the Prague Castle District.

As early as July 1917, in the month of his second engagement to Felice, Kafka sent a parcel of texts to his publisher. It contained thirteen prose pieces – the fruits of the previous winter – as well as the story "Before the Law", which stems from the unfinished novel *The Trial*, and which is also known as the "Legend of the Gatekeeper" or "Parable of the Gatekeeper". Kurt Wolff, the recipient of the package, was four years younger than Kafka and had begun his career in publishing together with Ernst Rowohlt in Leipzig.

Since 1912, he had been running the publishing house alone and under his own name. Wolff, who had a keen sense for great literature, not only published the works of Kafka, but also brought out books by Georg Trakl, Franz Werfel, and Heinrich Mann. While Kafka was revising the proofs of the *Country Doctor*, he had the idea of dedicating the book to his father. Any reader who knows of this difficult father-son relationship will be immediately struck by the two words "my father". In 1918, Kafka had written on the subject in a letter to his friend Max Brod.

"Since I decided to dedicate the book to my father, it has meant a lot to me that it should come out soon. It is not as if I could be reconciled to my father through it; the roots of this enmity go too deep here, but I would have done something; even if I hadn't emigrated to Palestine, I would at least have run my finger over it on the map."[9]

94

Left: The proof sheet shows the title page of the *Country Doctor* with corrections in Kafka's own handwriting.

Right: Kafka's father Hermann, to whom the *Country Doctor* is dedicated.

However, as the Kurt Wolff Verlag had to struggle with the problems of the war years, the collection of Kafka's short stories did not appear as quickly as he had hoped; it was first published only in 1920. This delay was probably of no significance at all to Kafka's father: he probably also disposed of this book, dedicated to him, with the short sentence which has come down to us through the *Letter to Father:* "Put it on the night table!"[10]

The stories themselves have one thing in particular in common: somewhere, whether at the beginning or later in the course of the text, an unsettling moment, which is sometimes termed the "Kafka Paradox", occurs. Readers can now puzzle over the significance of, for example, the fact that the country doctor suddenly finds pigs in the old stable, the reason why he only notices the patient's dreadful wounds on second glance, or why he suddenly lies down in bed next to the patient himself. There is no shortage of scholarly interpretations: does "riding" mean something along the lines of a "ride on the pen" and is "A Country Doctor" therefore about the act of writing itself?

Or can we make progress through the countless erotic allusions: the bed, the mine, the worms in the wounds? The enigmatic character of Odradek in "The Concern of the Head of a Family" would probably just react to such attempts at analysis with his rustling laugh, for the stories are like Odradek himself: they are "impossible to catch". They cannot be kept in any of the pigeonholes into which interpretation tries to force them because, at crucial points, the reality within the text does not correspond to the reality of the material world.

THE RECEPTION OF *A COUNTRY DOCTOR*

Although Kurt Wolff tirelessly advertised the *Country Doctor* in numerous catalogues and publications within the book trade, the book was at first an abject failure. "The lack of public success is evidence against the public. For these sketches of dreamlike events are that rarely successful attempt in German literature to describe the most abstract of things in the most concrete of terms,"[11] wrote a perceptive reviewer of the new publication in October 1920. Admittedly, individual stories from the volume were continually printed in various periodicals and even appeared in translation abroad. In Germany, however, the National Socialist regime prevented the circulation of Kafka's work, and even in Czechoslovakia, its reception was not established until the Kafka Conference in Liblice in 1963, as a consequence of which, Kafka even became a symbol of the "rebirth of intellectual and artistic freedom" after the Prague Spring of 1968.[12] The significance of Kafka's texts was recognized at an earlier date in other countries: *The Castle* was published in Great Britain and the US in 1930, *The Trial* in France, Norway, and Italy in 1933. Today his books have been translated into all major languages and it is astonishing how far the effects of the author reach: Kafka is extremely influential in modern Arabic literature for example.

The complexity of Kafka's stories also makes them ripe for adaption in other art forms. The German composer Hans Werner Henze (b. 1926) wrote, for instance, the radio opera *Ein Landarzt (A Country Doctor)* – an opera conceived for the radio rather than the stage that premiered in 1951. In the 1990s, several composers were inspired to make musical adaptations by the character Odradek, among them Gideon Lewensohn, for example, born in Jerusalem in 1954, and Michael Hirsch (b. 1958), a composer and actor based in Berlin. Several film directors have also been attracted by Kafka's texts so that, to date, there have been several films about the former ape Red Peter from "A Report for an Academy", for example, such as those by the Spanish director Carles Mire (1947–1993) in 1975 and Börje Ahlstedt (b. 1939) from Sweden only a year later. The Finn Katariina Lillqvist (b. 1963) made a puppet animation of *A Country Doctor*.

In May 1917, Kafka gave up writing in the Golden Lane "because of the beautiful weather and the difficulty in sleeping that goes with it".[13] A few years later he laid down in his will that all his manuscripts, "without exception and preferably unread", should be burned – with a few qualifications: "Of all that I have written, the only things that are valid are the books *Judgement, Stoker, Metamorphosis, Penal Colony, Country Doctor* and the story 'Hunger Artist'."[14]

However critical Kafka was of his own literary creations, the stories that arose in that wartime winter in the little house in the Castle District had validity for him. Once again the texts resemble Odradek: they will probably live on for eternity.

A scene from Katariina Lillqvist's puppet animation of *A Country Doctor*. The director spent time studying in the Czech Republic.

Note 1: Postcard to Felice, 7th December 1916. The letters and postcards to Felice Bauer are cited according to Franz Kafka, *Briefe an Felice und andere Korrespondenz aus der Verlobungszeit,* ed. Erich Heller and Jürgen Born (Frankfurt am Main, 1995).

Note 2: Although the edition is dated 1919, it did not appear until May of the following year.

Note 3: Letter to Felice, late December 1916/early January 1917.

Note 4: Letter to Felice, late December 1916/early January 1917.

Note 5: See Harald Salfellner, *Das Goldene Gäßchen* (Prague, 2000).

Note 6: Letter to Felice, late December 1916/early January 1917.

Note 7: Franz Kafka, *Briefe an Ottla und die Familie,* ed. Hartmut Binder and Klaus Wagenbach (Frankfurt am Main, 1974), pp. 32ff.

Note 8: "The monk's cell of a true writer", noted Max Brod in his diary in February 1917, after a visit to Kafka.

Note 9: Franz Kafka, *Briefe 1902–1924* (Frankfurt am Main, 1975), p. 237.

Note 10: Franz Kafka, *Brief an den Vater* (Prague, 2007), p. 52.

Note 11: Jürgen Born, ed., *Franz Kafka: Kritik und Rezeption zu seinen Lebzeiten 1912–1924* (Frankfurt am Main, 1979), p. 102.

Note 12: Ehrhard Bahr, "Kafka und der Prager Frühling", in Heinz Politzer, ed., *Franz Kafka,* 2nd edn. (Darmstadt, 1980), p. 517.

Note 13: Franz Kafka, *Briefe an Ottla und die Familie,* ed. Hartmut Binder and Klaus Wagenbach (Frankfurt am Main, 1974), p. 35.

Note 14: Letter to Max Brod, 29th November 1922.